Ashley's Tale

By
Mike Duke

Ashley's Tale
By Mike Duke

Copyright ©2018 by Mike Duke

Edited by Donelle Pardee Whiting

ISBN: ISBN-13: 978-1-945263-33-0

For distribution, please visit
www.stitchedsmilepublications.com
or email
distribution@stitchedsmilepublications.com

"I assess the power of a will by how much resistance, pain, torture it endures and knows how to turn to its advantage."
— *Friedrich Nietzsche*

The hand clamped over her mouth as she turned around, the other cupping the back of her head. The man pulled her in close with a violent jerk, bending down to place his eyes just above hers, locking her in his stare.

Everything came together in one overwhelming moment to infect Ashley with fear and establish the man's dominance—vicelike pressure restraining her skull from any movement, his suffocating proximity, and dead eyes staring down, holding hers captive. A car crash she never saw coming. That's how it felt. Too much to process at once. System overload. But then he spoke, and her bowels melted. She nearly pissed herself. His voice was little more than a whisper but harsh and cold, like gravel in winter mixed with a distilled malevolence. The intent of his words pierced and paralyzed her.

"Don't you fucking move a muscle, or I'll gut you right here. Do you understand?"

Ashley's eyes were blinds thrown wide, her pupils dilated from pure drops of terror. She nodded.

"Not one sound. Not a peep. Or I'll do far worse than rape you. You do understand."

It was a statement, not a question, but Ashley nodded again anyway. Her eyes blinked and tears began to stream down her face.

"Tears are irrelevant. I will not relent. Turn them off and play the part I command. You will go where I say go, arm in arm … like lovers." He smirked and let out a light chuckle. "We'll walk to your vehicle, and I will drive. Yes?"

She nodded once more, trembling beyond her ability to control. He removed the hand from her mouth and replaced it with a single finger.

"No noise."

Before she could do anything, he clinched a handful of hair, pulled her in, and kissed her, shoving his tongue deep inside to play about. Ashley pulled back, an instinctive act of resistance, but his grip was far too strong. All her limbs went weak and failed, yet still he held her up. Sensing her stomach churn, he pulled back, directing her head down, her knees collapsing to the ground as she vomited.

He brushed Ashley's hair back from her face and held it, his vice grip hands now gentle.

"Are you finished with your little spectacle of disgust?"

Ashley shook her head, spat on the grass. "I don't know … maybe."

"It profits nothing. That is simply your weakness on the ground. Leave it."

Still gripping a handful of hair, he lifted up in a firm, steady motion, beckoning her to stand.

"Now. Let's go."

He released her hair and hooked his left arm under her right arm and began walking. Ashley followed, compliant, the proverbial sheep to the slaughter.

His voice changed, softer but somehow more sinister, and he gestured with his free hand, a visual means to enhance the meaning of what his words expressed. Someone looking on would think them a couple and that he was serenading her with poetry perhaps.

"'Let us go then, you and I, when the evening is spread out against the sky like a patient etherized upon a table; let us go through certain half-deserted streets … that follow like a tedious argument of insidious intent to lead you to an overwhelming question … Oh, do not ask, 'What is it?' Let us go and make our visit.'"

They arrived at Ashley's car as he finished quoting T. S. Elliot. *The Love Song of J. Alfred Prufrock* passage skipped off her brain until he gave significant emphasis to the last two lines. A monstrous, playful emphasis.

"Are you ready to make our visit Ashley?" He patted her hand.

She stuttered, trepidation paralyzing her tongue, but managed to get a timid "Yes" out just before her brain asked the question—"how does he know my name?"

"You fucking Collaborator," he murmured.

His left arm dropped behind her, arcing up and then down like a scythe, the inner forearm striking the base of her skull.

Ashley saw a bright light, then gladly let the darkness envelope her.

*****

Ashley woke on her side in the trunk of her car, restrained and with duct tape across her mouth. Her hands were cuffed behind her and her feet were shackled. Another pair of cuffs connected the two chains, keeping her ankles cinched up near her buttocks. The vehicle drove on for some time. Helpless, she cried, a soft, whimpering lamentation.

In the dark she felt small and young again, lost in the black beneath her covers, waiting to be someone's plaything. The longer they drove, the deeper her mind burrowed. She imagined the steps outside her door, the creaking of hinges, and the weight of pressure on her bed. Her body had lain rigid, powerless to resist the sweaty palms caressing her face. The memories were poison, the kind that burns through a man's guts in searing agony.

Ashley screamed in desperation, unable to envision that life anymore, but was jolted with electricity an instant later, her neck folding sideways, pulled by the seizing muscles. It was then she realized something was around her throat, dragging her back into the present.

He put a fucking bark collar on me?! her mind screamed.

She pleaded in silence for her mother, for release, for the nightmare to stop, for mercy and a miracle from God— just like she pleaded long ago, only now she hoped it would be to some avail.

She was still lost in desperate supplication when the vehicle turned, stopped, and began backing up for some distance. It halted again, and she could hear some type of large bay door being raised with chains. Within a minute, the car had been backed in, and the door lowered.

They had arrived.

Dread excited Ashley's heart to pound, a careening rhythm of war drums trembling in her ears, commanding her to run. Incapable of fleeing, panic twisted her guts until they squeezed the bile to near overflow, burning her throat as the noxious odor permeated her sinuses. She tried to control her gag reflex. If she puked now it could choke her to death. She forced herself to breathe in through her nose at a controlled, steady rate then expel it even slower, thinking of someplace peaceful and beautiful, with rolling waves and birds making song. The trunk opened and a tidal wave crushed her vision of paradise.

The man looked down at her, his body all shadow in the low light.

"We're here," he chimed in a joyful tone then lifted her from the trunk. Without effort, he threw her over his shoulder where she writhed like a live pig on a spit, impotent to escape. He shut the trunk with his free hand then walked over to a wall, his gait casual, relaxed. There he flipped a switch. A single light came on. Ashley's eyes darted back and forth, trying to take in every inch of space the light unveiled.

There was her car and the bay door. Arcing her head upward, she could tell the ceiling was high and vaulted. As the man walked further away from the entrance, numerous tools, and various shop equipment came into sight amongst the shadows. They went through a door, banging her head off the doorframe. He turned and flipped another switch.

She could see a very polished concrete floor sloping down to a drain hole. Stainless counters lined two of the walls, immaculate and shining. One contained a sink. The walls were covered with sheets of light tan paneling, vinyl perhaps. He laid her down. The floor was remarkably cold for the first week of October. Ashley scanned the rest of the room. Multiple metal cases were stacked in one corner near a door.

It was then she saw the fourth wall, and her heart skipped a beat. It was covered from top to bottom with huge sections of mirror like you might find in a ballet school or yoga studio. A few feet away from it sat an odd contraption. The metal feet of four legs were bolted to the floor. On one side there was a platform midway up. The top of it was a form of leather saddle over padding perhaps, but was turned sideways to the mirror, not to ride but to lean over. There were manacles on each side, a set for both feet and hands.

A shudder wracked Ashley's body. The violation and abuse she suffered as a child seemed to pale in comparison to what she imagined was about to happen. He took the handcuffs off her wrists, removed the shackle chain, then helped sit her up. She rubbed her wrists and looked up at him. This was the first time she had seen him in good light. He was tall with a large, chiseled, muscular build, a trimmed beard, and black hair buzzed short. He had dark brown eyes and dark circles around them. His skin was weathered and scarred along one cheek. He wasn't quite handsome, but he wasn't ugly either. His attention was undivided, though.

11

He was focused on her and nothing else, a man of one solitary intent, and intent was displayed without ambiguity across his face. A shiver ran through Ashley's spine as she recognized his lustful desires peaking.

He stepped behind her and took the bark collar off then walked over to the wall in front of her.

"Yelling, screaming, crying out … none of that shit will help." He tapped the wall. "Soundproof sheetrock construction with vinyl noise barrier paneling covering it. *No* sound is escaping this room … you understand?"

Ashley looked up like a helpless lamb ready to be sheared by the shepherd, and not a bleating noise was made. She nodded, terrified to make him angry in any way. He tugged at the edges of the duct tape with a delicate pressure then peeled it off.

"Please don't hurt me" she whispered, looking down as she said it. He chuckled.

"Hurt? What is hurt? Words hurt the heart but not the flesh. You may punish the flesh but cannot always break the spirit. And if you heal up stronger than before, is it really hurt? Scar tissue is stronger than regular skin. Broken bones that have mended are stronger. Broken hearts though, how many ever recover? So, what is true hurt? Whatever breaks the spirit, pierces the heart, and crushes both. That's real hurt."

Ashley was confused. "What are you going to do to me?"

"I'm not sure yet. But you will choose. Every step of the way, you will choose." He smiled at her, some kind of twisted warmth spreading across his face; his eyes tasted her beauty, expressing a knowledge of things she did not know yet, things she did not want to know at all. Ashley recoiled. Realizing it was noticeable, she tried to minimize her reaction at the last second.

"It's ok, darling." He caressed her face. "The weak will perish, and the strong will thrive. Be strong."

He unlocked the shackles on her feet. Removing them, he plopped onto the floor between her and the mirrored wall, crossing his legs.

"Stand up," he said.

Ashley looked at him, her countenance full of apprehension.

"Come on," he insisted, lifting both hands in a repetitive upwards motion.

Ashley moved with a cautious trepidation, posting her hand on the floor then moving her leg back behind her to a kneeling position. Never taking her eyes off the man, she placed a hand on her knee to leverage herself up, a progressive climb to an erect back.

"Turn around." He gestured with his hand, finger pointing down tracing two circles in a row.

Ashley obeyed. Taking small, slow steps to turn until she faced him again.

"Jump up and down."

She hesitated but wasn't so self-conscious as to disobey. She jumped, just enough for her feet to leave the ground. She felt self-conscious when her breasts still managed to heave and bounce for him. Objectified and demeaned. The man was like a slave owner checking out the stock on display before purchasing.

"Twirl like a dancer," he said.

Ashley felt ungainly. She had never been one to dance, despite her athletic frame and pretty face. She almost stumbled as she tried to spin around the first time.

"Again."

The second time was better but still not smooth. She faced him once more.

"Hmmph." He scooted off to the side so the saddle contraption was straight ahead. "Go to the saddle. Lay over it and place your hands in the manacles."

Pleasantries were over it seemed. Down to business. Ashley was consumed by a growing panic. She wanted to flee but knew she could not escape, knew to try would bring severe punishment she couldn't even fathom. An acute dread gripped her. Frozen by the horrors to come, and her inability to do anything helpful on her own behalf, she simply halted in place. Her brain could not command. Her feet could not comply.

His tone was sharp as he barked, "Go!"

The edge in his voice broke the paralysis. She did not want to anger him further, to provoke a greater wrath and misery than he already had prepared. Obeisance was her sole hope of making it out alive.

She took her first step, feet heavy with fear. Another step, legs clumsy, weighted, as if the nerves were just waking up from an unwanted slumber. As she kept putting one in front of the other she grew more stable. The sight of her face in the mirror was unbearable and caused her to keep her eyes fixed on the floor. She arrived, leaned over the smooth, worn leather, considering the manacles dangling beneath her. She had to lean further over the top to reach them, offering up her buttocks at what she believed would be the man's hip level. She grabbed the manacles and fastened them onto her wrists one at a time, locking them in place. Then, she closed her eyes and waited, trying not to throw up again.

The man stood and walked over, pulled a pin and raised a small platform for her knees to rest on, then strapped her ankles down. Though her hands had enough excess chain to move back and forth a bit, the ankles were unable to budge at all. He moved in front of her and caressed both shoulders while allowing his groin to touch the top of her head and press down gently. Ashley stared at a mysterious, dark stain on the floor beneath her trying not to think about the bulge tickling her scalp. The man squatted, the crotch of his pants moving her long hair, then traced his fingers from her upper arm all the way down to her captive hands.

Without warning he seized both wrists and jerked up and down four times in rapid succession, screaming out loud as if he were expressing her unspoken desperation. The hopelessness of a weak and powerless victim awaiting their gluttonous abuser's every vice. He laughed at her, leaning back and tilting his head down to one side while still holding her wrists.

Ashley wouldn't bite and look up.

"C'mon, Ashley. I'm just giving voice to what your fear won't permit you to release right now. You're bracing for the inevitable, but like any good rollercoaster's first drop, screaming always makes it better."

He buried his face in her hair, breathed deep through his nose then exhaled with a pronounced, pleasant sigh. She smelled like jasmine and dread.

He stood with purpose and moved behind her.

"Ok, Ashley. It's time to choose."

He leaned against the crotch of her pants, pushed his hips forward and rested there for a few seconds, eyes rolled back, relishing the softness of her womanhood. Bending over her buttocks, he grabbed a handful of hair and pulled her head back, bringing her ear to his lips. The wetness of his hot breath made Ashley's skin crawl.

She cast her gaze about the room in a panic unable to avoid catching a glimpse of a face in the mirror, some stranger's face, her mind insisted. The stretched neck and hairline, eyes wild with a palpable fear … the absolute weakness. She told herself the horrific image couldn't be a reflection, but Ashley knew it was hers. It was identical to a younger face she saw in a dresser mirror years ago, on too many occasions, in fact, to deny what her brain would never forget.

"Choose what?" She labored to breathe, squeezing her eyes shut and trying not to cry. Her whole body trembled. The man chuckled at her distress.

"Do you want me to love you …" he released her hair and moved away, letting his hand caress her glutes. He picked up a light stick and thumped it in his hand once. "… or beat you?" He paused for several seconds, letting the weight of the moment settle on her with all its might.

She just cried and shook her head, unconsciously denying the reality of the moment.

"Well, sweet thing, what's it gonna be? We may have all day and night, but damn if I'm gonna waste my time twiddling my thumbs."

When she failed to respond, he slammed the stick down on the concrete floor in front of her face, just missing her head. A resounding THWACK echoed through the room. Ashley jumped as much as her body could move.

"Come on now, girl! If you don't pick one, then I'll have to … and I know what I would like to do." He moved behind her again, balanced the stick across her lower back, and gripped her waist, bumping her crotch with his own. "Come on, you've been a good girl just like this before … for Uncle Tim."

Ashley's head jerked about in an effort to look at him. "How do you know about that?" she exclaimed, pleading for an answer to this insanity.

"Aw, shucks, girl. I don't pick my women willy-nilly. I do my homework. I have criteria! *Preferences.*" The man snickered.

"Uncle Tim really fucked your head up good, didn't he? How many nights did he come in your room and tell you "shhhh" and promise you it was the right way for you to show your love for him? How many times did that sick bastard damage you physically, mentally, and emotionally? Did he threaten to hurt you or hurt your family? In all those years did he ever beat you? Did you ever try to tell yourself you liked it just to help you feel in control, or did it just make you feel violated, weak, and helpless and cause you to live every day of your *god-damned* miserable life in dread from then to now?"

The longer his monologue carried on, the more violent Ashley's weeping sobs grew until, at last, when he paused, she could take it no more.

"WHY ARE YOU *DOING* THIS TO ME?!" she screamed.

"Is that what you asked ole Uncle Tim?" His demeanor changed. He stared into her eyes, as if trying to see her soul, to reach something inside.

"Does the 'why' even matter? I am the *mighty* one here. You are the *weak* one. I can do as I please, and there is *none* who can tell me nay. I revel in your lamentations and get *high* on the power imbalance I hold over you. There is *nothing* you can say that holds authority over my strength or excuses your weakness."

Ashley's mouth hung in shock. She didn't know how to respond to this absurdity.

"Alright. Enough monologuing," he said, his tone impatient. "Pick your poison. The rod of flesh … or the rod of wood?"

"Damn you!" she screamed. "Why?! Why are you doing this to me, you *sick* fuck?!" She shook the whole saddle with a convulsive flurry of jerking movements, pulling against her bonds, while in her mind, memories of pulling against Uncle Tim's grip pinning her arms to the bed as she struggled to twist free pushed to the surface.

"Well, I guess it'll be the rod of flesh then …" He unzipped his pants with a quick flick of his wrist. The noise was like an arrow through her liver, debilitating, causing her to hyperventilate and shout out.

"NO! NO! For the love of God just beat me! Please! Please don't rape me! Please don't rape me. I can't go through that again. Please. Please don't." She dropped her head in defeat and continued to whisper "please." The man waited for what felt like an eternity before she heard the zipper again, returning to its closed position.

"OK then. You made a choice. Spare the soul and punish the body!" he exclaimed, like some southern preacher trying to rile the audience up. "Now we're getting somewhere."

He picked the stick up, hefted it, then let it sing through the air a couple of times. Ashley flinched, the speed of the stick's whooshing sound foretelling how painful the impact would be.

After a moment, Ashley heard a click, felt him grab the back of her shirt and lift up. The sound of fabric being severed was like nails on a chalkboard as the man's pocket-knife cut the shirt in half from hem to collar. He released his grip and the shirt fell off to each side, exposing her skin.

Folding the blade closed, he clipped it back in his front pants pocket. He placed both hands on the small of her back and traced the edge of her pants out to each hip, slipped his fingers in between her tender flesh and the material, then tugged and jerked, lowering Ashley's pants and panties down around her knees, together. His eyes wandered up to her exposed labia. He swallowed hard and sweat appeared on his brow, his gaze lingering as he stood erect and grabbed the stick again.

"This stick won't break anything where I'm going to hit you. But it's going to burn like hell itself. Gonna look like a demon's been clawing at you when I'm done. But flesh heals. Always remember that. Your flesh can heal up from almost anything that doesn't kill ya flat out. Remember that. And remember, this was your choice. Own it. Now," he paused for a second, "let's get this party started."

Without any other warning, he let the stick fly, cracking her in the ass. Ashley's head snapped up, and her whole body went rigid. Her face scrunched, screwing her eyes tight as she held her breath. The burn was immediate and overwhelming. She was whipped as a child a few times, but that didn't hold a candle to this pain. A dark red line appeared along her naked flesh, and the swelling wasn't far behind.

"Aaawww, yeah! That's what I'm talkin' about! Unnhh! I need a beer!"

He walked out of the room and returned seconds later cracking a cold one open and taking a sip. Ashley was focusing on breathing again, adrenaline and endorphins flooding her system from the pain.

"Alright! Now we're cooking with fire! Hold my beer and watch this, girl!" He put the beer in her right hand. "And take a sip if you like."

Her immediate thought was *fuck you!*, but then it occurred to her, anything that might help dull the coming pain was better than nothing. She turned the beer up as best she could and guzzled. He waited for her to finish before letting the stick fly again. This time on her thigh. Ashley yelped. Unable to stop herself, she started to cry, tears dropping to the floor, shaking from convulsive breaths, the pain too sharp.

"Bitch! You better not cry!" he shouted. "You hear me?"

He shot around and knelt in front of her, lifting her chin so she had to look him in the eye.

"Don't you dare scream or cry. You *want* to give me the satisfaction? Huh? You want to make me feel more powerful? Are you that frail? For Christ's sake, at least hold out longer than two hits before you squeal like a fucking little pig. You're *weak* and *pathetic*, Ashley." He spat those two descriptive words at her, disgust filling his face, nose wrinkled, upper lip rising in a sneer. "But if you got a lick of spine in you, that just might change."

Ashley's face was horrified and confused. She wanted to weep and wail, but she also thought he would want her to do so. She reasoned if she gave him what he wanted right away, he might stop sooner than later. She couldn't make sense of his actions. All she could do was try to obey, to brace herself and attempt to restrain any further cries.

He swung, landing on her ass again, in the exact same spot as before. The pain doubled and she hollered, more tears escaping eyes that begged for pity in the mirror.

"I said don't cry! I *promise* you, Ashley, I will *NOT* stop beating you as long as you are crying. Toughen up!"

SMACK!

The stick struck her in the back, directly over her ribcage. She couldn't scream. It stole her breath. Paralyzed her lungs.

The blows came rapid fire now. Back, lower back, glutes, thighs. He mixed them up, sometimes doubled up, the light stick flickering out to smite Ashley's tender skin. Welts were multiplying. Ashley never wept because she couldn't breathe.

And then, suddenly, it ended. Her chest heaved, struggling for air, dying to cry out, to weep, to sob without restraint. She bit her lip, kept her mouth shut, even once she could breathe normal again.

"Alright, Ashley. Well done. That was *so* much better. I'm actually proud of you, kid. You sucked it up and cowboyed up right well."

He walked over to a cabinet and retrieved something. When he returned, she felt a wet, cold drop on her skin. He started with her glutes and then methodically addressed every welt, rubbing in some form of gel.

"This is just aloe vera gel with a pain reliever added," he informed her.

At first it burned, but then the topical analgesic started to kick in, and Ashley began to find some relief. He put a thick gauze bandage over the welts on her butt, taping it in place. She felt the shackles loosen on her ankles, and then they were gone. He jerked her pants the rest of the way off. However, he repositioned her underwear along her hips. Ashley wondered why. Perhaps to help hold the bandage still.

He went to the cabinet again and returned with a hospital gown. After un-cuffing her hands, he allowed her to stand. While he pulled the ruined shirt off Ashley's arms, she met her own eyes in the mirror. She saw weakness, but a seed of strength as well, before averting her face. He moved in front of her and held the gown out. Ashley slid her arms through the holes. The man proceeded to tie it behind her back, then walked her to the door she had not seen opened yet. He turned the knob and pushed the heavy metal door. It swung inward on reinforced hinges.

"Go sit down while I get you something to eat," he said, kindness now filling his voice.

Ashley shuffled in, taking small steps so as not to stretch or rub the skin too much and lowered herself onto the bed in a seated position. The room was not what she expected. A nice, full-size bed sat low to the ground up against one wall, box spring and mattress only. It was made with silky sheets and a pretty comforter with large pink flowers. An additional blanket was folded on the bed.

The walls were covered with posters and magazine foldouts of women ... women fighters, some real, some fictional. Cynthia Rothrock movie posters, Kathy Long in kickboxing attire, and Ronda Rousey holding her belt were front and center, but there were others as well. Uma Thurman in *Kill Bill*, an old *Red Sonja* poster, and signed pictures of Lucy Lawless as Xena The Warrior Princess. There were also several pages from martial arts magazines showing sequences of self-defense moves being performed by women against larger males.

On the dresser were several books stacked together, amongst them: *The Gift of Fear*, Sun Tzu's *The Art of War*, Miyamoto Musashi's *Book of Five Rings*, and a biography of Joan of Arc. The man entered the room wheeling in a little table with food on it and pushed it up to her, the roller legs straddling her own. There was hot soup, a spoon, and napkins, along with a large glass of water. Off to the side was a single pill.

"The pill is for pain and to help you sleep. Eat. Tomorrow you will choose again."

He closed the door before she could say anything else. She listened to multiple clicks as deadbolts slid in place, and padlocks were closed. The sound of his feet retreating over concrete. Another door closed.

All was silence then. Ashley released a long, weak exhalation, her body breathing out the toxic anxiety that had gripped her since the moment the man seized her on the college campus. Her adrenaline levels had soared when she woke up in the trunk of her car. Until now they had maintained their high altitude. In the man's absence, though, her system bottomed out, hormone levels plummeted; the tension in her knotted muscles involuntarily collapsed.

Weakness consumed her. Ashley's whole body trembled. She leaned back against the wall on her bed and just breathed. In. Out. Repeat. Slower now. Repeat again.

In time she was able to hold her hands still enough to sip the soup he left behind. It was delicious. It took her stomach time to settle, but before long she was able to eat it all. She debated with herself over the pill, but the pain was too bad. Conceding at last, she took it then snuggled in under the covers, thinking of her mother until she cried herself to sleep.

*****

Ashley opened her eyes slowly, hoping the nightmare was just that, but it was not her bed, not her pillow beneath her head, and not her decorations on the wall. She turned over and started, her body jerking into motion with violent intensity. The man sat across the room in a chair, watching her, quiet as he sipped coffee.

"Fuck!" she spat and scurried to a seated position, back to the wall, covers pulled up to her neck. Her body shouted back at the startled movement, every welt and battered muscle highly discontent.

"Good morning." He took another sip then pushed the table over. "Peanut butter, honey, and toast, plus coffee and a pain pill. You need food but nothing heavy. We have much to do today."

"What do you mean?" she asked, while grabbing the coffee first, her shoulders rolled forward, voice low and timid.

"Let me explain." He spoke with clear and deliberate purpose, pausing where appropriate for emphasis and giving Ashley time to follow his logic.

"I am a man of … what shall we say? Unique desires. I live for the hunt, for competition. Stalking you and catching you was much more enjoyable than beating you last night. But even that took little effort because of how weak and oblivious you are. I abhor weakness, but abusing or killing the weak is no sport. Ease disgusts me just as much as weakness. If something is to be of any value it must require skill and discipline. *But*," and he held up one finger, "last night was *necessary* … for *you* to know *my* intent, my commitment to this process."

Ashley's head was spinning trying to understand.

"What process?" she asked, leaning back, an unconscious display of distrust, wary of what that one word implied and not sure she wanted to know the answer.

"The process of preparation. Of instilling a will to survive and fight in you and then putting it to the test … against me." He smiled, a wry, cunning expression that frightened Ashley.

Ashley sat dumbfounded. "Against you? How the hell could I ever stop you? You're *literally* twice my size or more."

The man chuckled then lifted his hand palm up and swept it across the room, indicating all the posters and pictures on the wall.

"There are ways. Every human being has vulnerabilities." He indicated each one with his free hand as he listed them. "Eyes. Larynx. Knees. Base of Skull. Even a smaller opponent can overcome with fury, violence of action, and attacking what is vulnerable. But even better …" He reached behind his back and withdrew a large knife and set it on her table, paused, and looked her in the eye as he slid it towards her, then pulled his hand away and set back in the chair.

Ashley stared at it. "I don't know how to use that," she said, a blunt admission of ignorance.

The man laughed, loud and brash.

"Grip it tight, preferably with the blade pointing down. Stab vital areas: throat, heart, descending aorta, femoral arteries, subclavian artery, lungs, liver, kidneys."

He indicated each one in succession by touching the location on her body.

"Stab repeatedly till they die. How complicated is that?" He paused, sipped his coffee, and stared at her, the question still poised by his expression. "This is the most fundamental use of the blade," he continued, "but there is a finer skill to be had as well. Or perhaps a garrote to choke your opponent with." He pulled out a long piece of 550 cord, high tensile strength synthetic fibers used by military for securing gear and a hundred other applications. He tied each end of the cord to two metal carabiners. Gripping one in each hand, he demonstrated wrapping it around an imaginary neck and cinching it up to strangle the victim.

"Or a bow and arrow, or gun to maintain distance and safety while you kill. Killing is a thinking man's game. The brutish know nothing beyond the simplicity that works on the weak and unprepared. But you, you must first learn the will to live, which means the will to kill, and then you must understand that the will to prepare to kill is even more important to survival." He stood up. "Now eat that sandwich and get dressed." He indicated a stack of clothes on a dresser. "I will provide this light breakfast each day for training, but you must acquire all else yourself."

He stepped forward, grabbed the knife, and returned it to its sheath, shaking his head as he walked out. "I'm disappointed in you, Ashley," he called over his shoulder. "I hoped you would attack me with it. In due time, perhaps."

Ashley looked at the sandwich and clothes. Her head spun, and her body ached, but she wasn't dead yet. *The living always have a chance the dead never get.* The thought popped into her head out of nowhere, remembering something she had read somewhere that basically said what she thought.

*****

Ashley walked out of her living quarters after using the attached bathroom and stood in front of the wall size mirror, assessing herself. Her figure was lean and fit, curvaceous in the right places, even showing through the sweat pants and pullover hoodie she wore. Long, dark brown hair was a tangled nest of bed head. She took the brush he left for her and worked through it with hurried strokes. It was an oddly plain brush, she thought, made from one solid piece of black plastic with plain black bristles. It didn't look like a normal woman's brush.

Her skin was spotless, lips a natural pinkish hue, and her lashes long. She wore little makeup if any at all. A soft face with a mousy nose and mouth and doe eyes made her a natural beauty. None of the welts were visible, she noted. She tucked the brush in the large hoodie pocket and shifted back and forth, feeling out the shoes he gave her, then stretched a little, trying to get her body to agree with movement. When done, she turned and walked towards the bay area, cautious as she approached the entrance. She found the door already propped open, awaiting her.

When Ashley stepped out into the large space, she could see far more than last night. There were a couple of cars in different states of repair, equipment and machines with functions unknown to her, but what surprised her the most was an octagonal cage, maybe 15 feet across, with a matted floor. A gated entrance sat wide open, inviting her to enter. The man stood within, leaning on the far side.

"Come in. Time for your first lesson."

Ashley proceeded to the gate, hesitated at the entrance, looking in and assessing the thick chain linked wire wrapping the metal framework.

"Come on," he waved her in. "Don't be scared to learn."

She stepped inside and walked to the middle.

"Attack me," he said, stepping away from the cage. "Like you want to kill me."

She stood there, looking him over. He was mere feet away, feet spread shoulder width, hands at his waist, thumbs tucked in his beltline. She stared at his crotch for a brief moment, then launched a kick at it as if she were kicking a soccer ball back in her youth. He dropped an arm down, intercepting the kick and scooping it off to the side. It left her off balance and vulnerable.

"Good. But don't stare at the target. You told me where you would attack. Look me in the eye and do it."

Ashley stared him in the eye and after several seconds of waiting, launched another kick at his groin but with the other leg. He only had time to jam it with his arm but not deflect it. She was left balanced and squared up to him, but she retreated. Her shin smarted a little bit from the contact with his ulna. Although it had been years since she played soccer and her body was fully conditioned to bone on bone contact, she hadn't lost all that toughness.

"Better. But the groin is a distraction, not the kill. You gotta follow up. You must never stop till you have finished your opponent. Deceive him at the onset, then attack with the fury of a wild beast, yet also employing a cunning intellect."

The last attack felt good. Ashley was starting to feel the aggression grow inside her. All the frustration over the last several hours building to a head.

"How am I supposed to do that?" she inquired.

"You must make them think one thing while you do another. Get them to buy into ..."

Ashley inched her way a little closer as he began talking, then, without telegraphing her intent, launched her foot forward as fast as she could, cleanly striking him in the groin. She immediately went for his eyes with both hands clasping his temples, thumbs digging for his eyeballs.

He almost looked startled, teeth gritted, head jerking back but there was no panic, only a calm, calculated response. Soaking the groin kick with little effect, he had closed his eyes instinctively. As Ashley clawed for them now, he grabbed both her wrists. Pushing her hands away from his face, he laughed.

"Good! Good!" he shouted. "That's what I want to see. *Fire! Wrath!*" The man's face was ebullient, full of pure delight with Ashley's aggression. She had gone for the kill, at least as much as she understood to.

Ashley struggled to pull her hands free, but he held tight. She launched a knee towards his groin, but he deflected it with his own knee coming across. She tried with the other knee, and he jammed it as well.

"Good. And against an untrained man that would probably have worked. But you must be better than that to present me with a challenge. You must be able to negate my strength. I must not be allowed to hold you and control your movements. Circle your right hand up and over my wrist." She did so. "See how I can't hold on? Now, circle it under and then over the top ... same effect, though in a different way."

He grabbed her wrists again. "Now. Free both your hands!" Ashley twisted and circled her hands under and over, breaking free. Without hesitation, she attacked his eyes again. He shrugged his shoulder and ducked away, deflecting her hands away from his face then stepped in and used his whole body to knock her back. She stumbled but regained her footing.

"Very good! Now let's begin teaching you all the tricky ways to keep someone from holding onto your arms."

They spent hours training, the man forcing her to maintain an intense pace. First the grab counters, then basic striking. He taught her to strike the throat with a "C" hand, letting her practice on his forearm. Elbows she practiced on his chest and then his forearms. Forearm hammers and clothesline techniques that would target the base of the skull she delivered to his chest and upper arms. Finger Jabs to the eyes were lightning fast, and he slipped his head off line as she delivered each one with malicious intent. Low line straight kicks meant to hyperextend the knees he had her practice on the cage itself.

He taught her how to generate power: stepping into her strikes, driving through with her hips, raising and lowering her center as necessary, and pulling people into her strikes. She took to it well, understanding and applying the principles and techniques in a short timeframe. Plus, Ashley's muscles were naturally fast-twitch, able to explode into action in an instant. Her movements came with greater speed and force once she learned a technique.

At last, they took a break. Her body was sore and stiff, but she knew staying active would keep it far less so than if she just sat down and did nothing. She hydrated again and kept stretching while she waited for the next lesson.

The man was a mystery. She wanted to ask him how he could invest so much time in teaching her only to want to hurt her. But she knew he would not answer, or he would say something as simple as, "because I can." She looked up from stretching and was surprised to see what he was doing. He was lifting a pig carcass up on a chain hoist, its hind legs spread with a hook through the hollow skin between bone and tendon on each side, a solid piece of steel connecting the two hooks preventing it from spinning wildly. The dead creature was hairy and large but not the size of hogs she had seen on a farm as a girl during a one of her field trips.

"What's that for?" she asked, ignorance breeding wariness.

"You must learn to kill with the blade. This is the first lesson. Come here."

He waved her over. She stood and closed the distance. He held the knife in his hand, the blade facing down. It was large, maybe twelve inches overall. The blade was fat in the middle and tapered spear-like to the point. Both edges were sharp. He demonstrated as he spoke.

"Grip the handle tight in your right hand, blade down, like you would use an ice pick, but place your thumb over the top of it as a cap to help prevent it from sliding if you hit bone or something else hard. Take a step back with your right leg, turning your body away from the opponent. Hide the blade along your arm, tip up, and behind your leg, arm at your side. This will help if you need to deceive someone. If you are hiding in wait or sneaking up on them, you can hold it near your jawline, point facing forward, ready to stab. When you stab, stab fast and hard, let the blade bury into the body up to your hand."

There was a thud as his hand hit the ribcage, but the blade didn't make a discernible sound.

"Pull it out and repeat till they stop fighting and stop breathing. If you are stabbing the gut, you can go quite fast, cycling your arm back and forth to stab two or three times per second."

He changed targets and sped up, the blade a blur as he drove the metal into the hog's abdomen faster than Ashley could count.

"But if you are stabbing through the rib cage be a

little more deliberate in targeting so you don't lose your blade skipping off a bone or withdrawing it on a bad angle." He slowed the pace down and made sure it went in and came out without hurrying too much.

"Once inside the body, you can also shove and jerk the handle back and forth to shift the blade around and cause even more damage. This is especially useful after stabbing the heart. Or, once you stab, you can grab it with both hands and rip down using the backside edge to rip through the flesh and manipulate your target." He paused for a moment and looked at her. "Your turn." He laid the blade down on a table and stepped several feet away.

Ashley approached the blade with a little trepidation but the last few hours had shown her she could do far more than she ever thought she could. She picked up the blade in her right hand, gripping it as he had shown, and approached the pig carcass. She assumed a stance, right leg back for power. The body of the pig was already full of stab marks and bleeding, a couple of the puncture wounds in the belly had portions of intestine pushing through. She breathed deep and launched herself forward, driving the blade between two ribs. It slipped through the leathery hide without any noticeable resistance. The bottom of her hand impacted its still warm flesh. She could hardly believe how easy it was.

She withdrew and repeated, again and again. She shifted to targeting the belly and stabbed as fast as she could in succession. In no time, she was breathing hard but somehow, she felt empowered.

"Now try it with a backhand motion. Like this." He folded his arms and then flickered his right hand out, palm down, simulating having a blade.

Ashley nodded then followed his instructions. *My god, that's fast*, she thought. She delivered several rapid

31

backhand stabs up and down the body of the pig then shifted back to a forehand power strike one last time, burying it again. She turned and looked at him, a true smile of satisfaction at learning something that empowered her appearing on her face, despite the rest of her circumstances.

He smiled back.

"Good. Very good!" He clapped for her. "Now, put the knife on the table and step away. I'll show you some more options."

Ashley pulled the blade out in a flash then held it at her side as she walked to the table, never taking her eyes off the man. *He's too far away*, she thought as she laid the blade down and backed away.

He approached and proceeded to skin the boar in silence, his every cut efficient, performed with an economy of motion. Once done, he motioned for her to come closer and look. She moved to where she had a better view.

"You see, the hide of animals offers far more resistance than the skin of men. We are simply meat, without any natural defense, just as now all you see is the pig's meat exposed without his hide. The blade is powerful. The edge and point are like magic, penetrating and opening the flesh with little effort. Observe."

He held the blade in a forward grip, like holding a hammer, and proceeded to press the point against the flesh. He pushed very easily, and the blade slid right into the torso as if it were butter. He then withdrew it, chose another location, and did it again.

"Slashing is no different." He made several short and smooth slashing motions across the flesh. Each time the meat parted.

"So, if you are cutting something that is close to the surface, it does not take much force at all."

His blade flickered out with speed rather than power, the point piercing the side of the throat where the jugular vein runs. He retracted the blade just as quick. Blood began to flow an instant later.

"See?"

Ashley was surprised again at how helpless the flesh was against the blade, even with so little force.

"Now, if we add force, the penetration of the slashes increases." He let one go along the rear leg thigh. It cut all the way to the bone. "Now you experiment." He laid the blade back down and stepped away to his previous position.

Just as he demonstrated, Ashley went through the motions, discovering the truth for herself. As she slashed the neck, more blood flowed. When she showed proficiency, he spoke up.

"Now slash the neck, hard!"

She did, and it cut to the vertebrae.

"Again!"

She sliced through it again in the same location, and it hung at an odd angle.

"Now from the backhand angle. Finish the job!"

Blood was flowing now, a torrential waterfall cascading to the concrete floor. Ashley obeyed and let the blade fly on the backhand. Once, twice, then one final forehand slice. The head fell, splashing her legs with blood as it poured from the stump. The large blade made quick work of the pig's neck.

The man clapped and laughed.

"Outstanding Ashley! Out-standing!"

"Now, final lesson for today. There is a small boar outside in a fenced in area. It weighs around fifty pounds and has no tusks yet, but it can bite. It is fast and strong and can take much punishment and trauma and still keep fighting, just like a man who is desperate to live can. You must

33

take that blade and kill it if you wish to eat."

"What?" was her reflexive response. "You want me to kill some little pig? *Why?*"

"It is the first step in learning the willingness to kill a man. Plus, if you wish to eat, you must kill. How do you think bacon winds up on a plate? Someone had to kill it for you. Now, you must do it for yourself. That is survival."

"You son of a bitch!" Ashley put her hands on her waist, the knife pointing toward him. "And what if I refuse to do it?"

"Well, if you are going to recover from your injuries and training and actually become a challenge for me you will need sustenance. So, if you refuse to do what is necessary to help achieve my goals ... well, I'll have to give you some motivation."

"Let me guess," Ashley said, anger edging her voice, "either I kill the pig, or you rape me. Is that my 'choice' tonight?" She made the bunny ear quotation marks as she said choice.

"How did you ever guess?" he smiled. "First, put the blade down and come over here."

Ashley knew it was pointless to fight at this point. She needed more skills to kill him. She couldn't pull it off right now unless he were asleep. She sat the blade down and walked right up to him.

"Turn around," he said, and she obeyed. He picked up a collar and wrapped it around her neck. It fit snug but didn't hurt. She felt him buckle it behind her neck and put a small padlock on it.

"Bark collar again?" she said, her sarcasm obvious.

"Actually, it's the kind that shocks the shit out of you if you go beyond the bounds of the property. So, don't think about running off. It'll keep shocking your sweet ass till you come back. Now, you're going to go through that door into the pen. I'm going to release the pig, and you're gonna kill it. Sweet and simple. Copy?"

She nodded begrudgingly.

"Alright. Go grab the knife, and then go through the door." He indicated which door. Ashley did as told. He shut and locked the door behind her then stepped outside to release the pig.

Ashley stood waiting across from where the pig would enter. The pen was a little bigger than the cage they practiced in, maybe twenty feet across. She clenched the blade's handle in the ice pick grip, held down by her leg. As she watched the man shift the pig into position for release, her adrenaline began to dump.

Her hands trembled. Her breathing came faster and a bit deeper, chest rising and falling on a steady, visible interval. Her skin went pale, and her stomach felt like a pit had opened up inside it as the blood was pulled away and pushed into skeletal muscle, preparing the body for what she would have to do.

The small gate raised, and the pig burst into the pen and made a beeline sprint for her. Even though it didn't have its tusks it acted like it did, trying to ram its head into her upper thighs and groin to tear at the femoral arteries. It startled Ashley, and she stepped offline just before it plowed into her, stabbing the pig's neck as she pivoted her whole body on the outside foot. She didn't think about it. Between the training earlier and pure survival instinct kicking in, it just happened.

It was a good blow, but not a killer. She kept stabbing and circling as it tried to turn the corner on her. Her third stab got lucky. It severed the spine halfway down. The pig's rear legs went limp, paralyzed. It squealed in pain and terror, trying desperately to pull itself away from Ashley, front legs digging into the ground, but with little success.

The man yelled. "Get it, Ashley. Stab it behind the shoulder, and drag that piggy down on its side."

Ashley listened and slipped around to its left side and hammered the blade into the body on its right side. She grabbed the blade with her left hand to reinforce and pulled the animal onto its left side.

"Now put your right knee on its body and pin its head. Then stab its neck and heart!"

Ashley brought her right knee up onto the pig's mid back as she pinned its head with her empty hand, obeying the man's coaching. It was solid muscle beneath her, but half of its body wasn't functioning, the half that could give it mobility, more drive to torque and twist and resist Ashley's body weight. Crippled, all it could do was try to thrash its head and gnash its teeth at her. Ashley struggled to keep the head in place, afraid if she didn't, it might rear its head and bite her face.

"Don't be so focused on defense that you don't attack!" the man yelled at her. "Stab that motherfucker!"

Ashley thrust the blade into the animal's chest, using it as another means of holding the pig down temporarily. It cried out from the injury, an almost human sound, announcing bloody murder to all its companions held nearby.

The pig was bleeding everywhere. Her free hand was covered with blood from her first blow to the neck. It slipped about, frantically searching for some solid purchase which she could grasp and leverage to effectively restrain the head. In a moment of desperate improvisation, Ashley grabbed the pigs ear, digging two fingers down into the canal and twisting its folds in between her other fingers in a claw-like grip. Holding on with a singular focus, she pushed the pigs head into the dirt and held it there.

She raised the knife high and drove it through the chest wall again. The pig squealed louder than before.

The blade rose and fell again, this time in the neck. Arterial spray shot through the air as she withdrew the blade and the squeals became high pitched gurgles. She kept stabbing, as fast as she could slam it in, pull it out and repeat, just like she had stabbed the carcass earlier.

The more holes, the faster it bled. Its struggles became feeble, what vigor it once had, now soaking into the soil.

The life is in the blood, Ashley remembered, a random intruding thought drawn up from the recesses of her brain under the influence of a massive adrenaline rush. *And so is the will and the strength to fight*, she thought as well.

In less than a minute, it stopped moving. Its breathing was weak and labored now—raspy gasps and rattling exhalations as its body fought to live despite the severity of its wounds. A collapsed right lung only made its efforts more futile. Another minute and its last breath hissed from between crimson stained teeth.

By the end, Ashley's stabs slowed from fatigue. She realized the pig was no longer breathing and gave it one last thrust to the heart to be sure, leaving the blade inside and jerking it back and forth as she gasped for air, her body trying to get more oxygen to fuel the muscles that no longer wanted to obey her mental commands.

She pulled the blade out and rolled off onto her back, staring at the blue fall sky, arms and legs spread wide, breathing deep the crisp, cool air. Exhausted beyond anything she had ever experienced, she felt alive, sick, and strong all at the same time.

Then she smiled wide as she thought, "*I'm sure as fuck not getting raped tonight.*"

*****

Ashley was allowed to shower and change clothes before he brought her back outside. The pig was already cut into smaller portions, dressed out, and sizzling on the grill. He put the collar on her once again then led her to a chair sitting across from his own, the grill beside him, and a small campfire in between them. Ashley plopped down, fatigue and soreness setting in. It was good to relax, but she had been thinking in the shower about stuff she heard and read in the past, like how to make yourself more of a real person to a captor, making it harder for them to dehumanize and kill their victim. She decided to try conversation with the man while she waited for the pig to cook, and he seemed amenable after her success today.

"So, you know my name is Ashley Wendell. I'm betting you know about my whole family: my mother and father, Claire and Matt Wendell, and my older sister Katrina. But you haven't told me your name yet."

A smile crept across his face. He took a sip of beer then reached in a cooler, pulled out another one, and tossed it to Ashley. She caught it and popped the top on the Bud Light can, thanking him as she did.

"So, you want to know my name, huh? Well, considering I reckon you won't ever leave here, it couldn't hurt. Name's Jacob. You can call me Jake."

Ashley cringed inside more than outward at the future threat but made herself smile anyway.

"Jake. Alright ..." She gulped twice at the can. "You know, Jake, I was raised out in Oregon. My daddy used to take us out in the woods camping sometimes when I was young. This kind of reminds me of those times," she lied.

"Hanging around a fire with me after everything that's happened in the last twenty-four hours reminds you of camping with your daddy as a kid? Wow. You are more fucked up than I thought." He gave a big belly laugh and slapped his leg. "C'mon Ashley. Don't bullshit da man with some hostage/captor psychological mind meld ploy."

Ashley felt the "oh shit" moment of being caught in the act and decided not to deny it.

"Well, I just want you to know who I am. I don't want to be dehumanized, depersonalized, and have my voice silenced and my life never mean anything. I have an identity, an intellect, a soul."

"Shit!" he sputtered. "You got chemicals fizzing between your ears like the rest of us, and yours ain't no better than others. There ain't no soul in either of us. Just atoms. No right. No wrong. Except what we think it is. It all comes down to might. Might makes right. And right now I got the might, and you don't. So, spare me any psychoanalysis. I've worked my way through that shit on my own."

Jake stood and turned to the grill, brushed more BBQ sauce on the meat, then pulled a few slabs off, slapping them on a plate with some pan cooked potatoes sautéed in olive oil.

"Eat up," he said, handing the plate to Ashley. "You're gonna need your strength tomorrow. Training all day, and you'll have to kill your dinner again."

He turned around and dished himself up. Sitting down in his chair, he devoured his meal. The two sat in silence, the fire light dancing off their faces, eating Ashley's kill.

*****

The following weeks bled into each other. The physical intensity was taxing and having to learn, process, and perform on short deadlines and under pressure was beyond challenging; Ashley had little time to feel. If she was not training, killing another pig, or eating, she was trying to stay awake. When she reached the point of severe fatigue each evening, he gave her caffeine pills, making her read the books on her dresser until she could not stay awake. She was immersed in violence by force, in every manner imaginable, pushing the limits of what the human spirt could endure. Still, she knew not to question or disobey his commands. It was learn to kill or become a fuck toy.

Jake taught her to fight like a devil with skill.

From reading body language and environment for intent and pre-assault indicators to verbally enforcing boundaries. She also learned to take preemptive action and attack first whenever possible. He even taught her deceptive tactics, stealth and how to sneak up on a man to take him out. Striking with maximum power generation to a target's vulnerable areas was a key area of training but knowing how to deal with counters was critical to success. She needed to be able to defend and counter when attacked.

Jake taught her how to be fast and efficient on her feet, how to manipulate the body, to grapple standing up and throw as well as prevent being taken down. He taught her how to fight on the ground with both traditional techniques and brutal moves that would never be allowed in a competition setting. They also covered basic escape and evasion tactics, which included defeating zip ties and handcuffs, plus picking locks.

Once she learned something new it was hours of repetition, drilling the moves, then executing them against random counters or with modifiers that made things more difficult. Always, Jake pushed her to finish him. Several times, he had to work hard to stop her from choking him or breaking his arm or leg. She was a quick study and desperation was driving her towards greater success every day.

She particularly took to the blade but was also getting very good at the use of the garrote and bow and arrow. Jake had to pull a real knife once and nicked his neck getting the blade in between his flesh and the 550 cord to prevent her from killing him when, without warning, she decided to go for broke. He had not punished Ashley for her efforts, to her great dismay. He just laughed and coughed and told her, "Good one, girl!"

Some nights, after she had worked harder than usual during the day, he allowed her to take down the pig with the bow and finish it with the blade. She had hit some of them as far out as 25 yards right through the heart.

Ashley was beginning to feel quite proud of her accomplishments, her confidence reaching higher levels each day. The longer her training went on, the less fear she felt. She even began to entertain thoughts of killing Jake and getting the fuck out of there.

He also taught her some basic Bushcraft—making fires, use of tools for various tasks, constructing temporary shelters, gathering and purifying water, land navigation, tracking and stalking. He made her sleep outside overnight using what she had learned when it got cold, and cook her food in the earth when a campfire might give her away. During these times, the collar was ever present to keep her in check, but he would sneak up on her with night vision goggles to observe her progress and see how light of a sleeper she was.

One night, he crept up to Ashley's lean-to shelter while she slept and took the knife he had given her for cutting and whittling. He had scolded her in the morning for not keeping it on her body. The next time she repeated her error, Jake secured the blade and pounced on her in the dark, still wearing the night vision goggles, straddling her chest and attempting to choke her. Before Jake could secure his position, she violently bucked her hips in an effort to roll him off. He felt it coming, though. Letting go of her throat he posted out, placing one hand on the ground to prevent her from reversing him.

He felt her arms move and sensed her right hand coming up and over his shoulder towards his head. He shrugged, reflexively protecting his neck and raising his left arm up as he turtled his head and moved lower on her chest. Something hit his skull. It struck hard and burned. He grabbed her wrist and pulled her arm across her body, rolling her on her stomach and pinning the weapon hand to the ground.

Looking down, he could see the punji stick she had made.

She set a trap for me, he thought. "You sly bitch," he said out loud as he pinned her arm with his knee and punched the back of her hand until she let go. He took it from her a mere moment before she could turn into him enough to reach it and switch hands. She spun her lower body beneath him, shooting her legs up to wrap around his chest and face. Her legs knocked the night vision goggles off his face as she isolated his arm, extending it the length of her torso in an attempt to break his elbow with her hips.

Since Jake no longer possessed the advantage of the night vision goggles, darkness worked equally against them both. It was all feel now.

Jake felt a pop in his elbow and scrambled to stack her lower body before she could do more serious damage. Folding her knees toward her face and putting all his weight on her, he smashed her as flat as possible. Four quick jerks, and he pulled his arm free from between her legs. He grabbed the waist of her pants, snatched up hard, flipping her over to land face down on the forest floor. Ashley was temporarily stunned and disoriented, deprived of any visual reference point. Jake seized the opportunity and proceeded to drag her backwards by her feet till she was stretched out.

He pounced on her back. Even as Ashley attempted to get to her knees, he hooked his feet around her hips, in between her legs, pressing his own hips down as he extended his legs and flattened her to the ground. She tried to push up with her arms but it was futile. Jake grabbed a handful of hair and pushed her head down, bending her neck forward to expose the base of the skull. He dropped a forearm right along the occipital line, knocking her unconscious but not inflicting any real harm.

Ashley slumped to the ground, all resistance ceased.

Jake withdrew a small flashlight and shined it around, locating the night vision goggles. He grabbed them, put them on again, then stood and backed away, fingering the bleeding wound on the back of his head.

Jake was lucky tonight. He had just barely avoided getting it in the neck. Ashley moaned and began to curl up in the fetal position, holding the back of her head.

"Very good, Ashley!" he yelled. "Very good, indeed! I'm impressed. I think you are ready for the next stage."

He turned around and walked away, happy as a kid with a new toy.

*****

In the morning, Ashley made her way back to the building and went to her room. The key to the collar was on her dresser. After unlocking it she showered. Jake had the standard fare of peanut butter and honey toast available but added a protein shake as well. She scarfed it all down then met him at the cage.

She smiled in deviant pleasure when she saw he had shaved a patch of hair and was wearing a small bandage where she had stabbed him the night before. He slipped a beanie over his head, having let Ashley see her handiwork before covering it up.

"That one took some super glue to fix," he said as she walked into the cage. "Nice job." He held out a fist bump and she bumped his hand without thinking about it. Feelings of pride overwhelming hatred for the moment.

"So. Next level. We're gonna up the ante."

Jake grinned while Ashley's face showed concern, but she didn't say a word. He grabbed a small remote from on top of the cage and pointed it at a timer on the table nearby.

"I'm setting the timer for one minute. If you can keep me from getting in your pants or knocking you out for one minute, you win. If I succeed, I'm going to rape you."

Ashley kept a straight face, but her heart skipped a beat, and she swallowed hard.

Jake stared at her, a matter of fact expression on his face. "You understand the rules?"

Ashley responded through clinched teeth. "Yes."

"Alright then. Let's get it on!" he shouted as he pumped his arm like the referees on the UFC. He pushed the button on the remote and sat it up on the cage in a safe spot then stepped back and waited for the buzzer.

Ashley's heart raced, adrenaline coursing through her system. She took two deep, controlled breaths, and the buzzer sounded.

Jake exploded, closing the distance and taking away Ashley's potential to kick his knee. He flickered out a left finger jab to her eyes in an attempt to distract her from his real goal, grabbing her hair with the other hand. She parried the finger jab hand away from her face as she stepped on a slight angle to her right, penetrating deep to bring her body alongside Jake's. One more step to his back and her hair was out of reach. She tried to get behind him, but he stepped out and circled. Ashley scrambled to wrap her arms around his torso and tucked her head behind his left shoulder. If he continued to circle he wouldn't be able to square up to her now, she could hang on and move with him. He was too big for her to connect her hands so she grabbed the clothing under the armpit furthest from her and his belt at the right rear hip. She pulled herself tight to him, like a spider monkey attached to his side and back, hanging on for dear life until she could find an opening to exploit.

Jake turned in a circle, trying multiple times to get his left arm around far enough to peel her back toward the front. Ashley held her position though and rode out his flurry of activity. When she felt his efforts subside, she hooked his leg with her own and kicked out, taking him down to his side. She released the belt and dug her fingers into his eyes. Peeling his head back by leveraging his orbital bones, she kneed him in the base of the skull twice. She was drawing back for a third knee when Jake turned into her and punched her dead in the solar plexus, knocking her off him. She flew back several feet before landing on her ass. She posted both hands on the floor behind her hips to stay erect and in the fight.

Ashley wheezed, desperate to fill her lungs with air again. The wind knocked out of her, she struggled to breathe, struggled to even continue on. The feeling was debilitating. She wanted to give up, but she could see Jake recovering from the knees to his skull. He shook his head and tried to get to his feet but was too dizzy. For a moment, Ashley thought she had won, her fear abating, but Jake wasn't giving up. He crawled towards her now, closing the distance in the time it took her to wheeze once more.

Ashley's body said no to fighting. A part of her brain, demoralized and dejected, said give up and let him have his way. But Ashley's spirit was a warrior now. Her will screamed a rebel cry. She wasn't going to be a volunteer victim, a collaborator in her own demise, as Jake had said to her that first night. He was going to have to fight her every step of the way if he wanted to get in her pants.

Ashley dug deep. The instant his face got close to her feet she cocked a leg and lashed out, kicking him in the cheekbone with her heel. As she planted the kicking foot on the floor, the other foot shot out to land another blow to his face. Jake blocked it and wrapped his arm around her leg. She tried to kick with her free leg. He blocked and wrapped that one as well. Pulling her lower legs together, he hugged them tight, both arms circling under her legs, then laid his chest against her knees. Her legs were isolated and controlled, trapped beneath his body.

Ashley scrambled to pull her feet out even as she struggled to catch her breath. She looked at the timer. Thirty seconds left. Jake began to take one arm out at a time and reinsert it further up under her thighs, then repeat on the other side, crawling up her legs and controlling her lower body the whole way as he cleared the cobwebs from his head.

He made it to her waist, and Ashley started striking him in the head. First where she had stabbed him, then returning to the base of the skull. Jake picked up his head and swung an open palm for her face. She saw it coming. Tucking her chin and shrugging her shoulder at the last moment, she caught it to her skull instead of her jaw. She took the hit. Despite the jarring shock and still trying hard to get more oxygen into her lungs, she went on the offensive once more. Grabbing Jake's face with both hands, she dug her thumbs into his eyes. Jake closed them, squinting hard, then shook his head back and forth to buy himself time and reduce the chance of Ashley doing real damage. She had him in a difficult spot.

If he let go of her legs, she would be free. If he didn't, she might actually dig an eye ball out. Jake decided to release her legs and grab her hands, but as soon as he did, she leaned back and pulled her feet in. She kicked out against his chest, right then left, breaking his grip and knocking him back a bit. She needed to launch him though, create some real space.

Ashley pulled both legs in and double kicked, hitting him high on the chest with the bottoms of her feet. It sent him flying backwards. He landed sitting on his butt. As he leaned forward to come back, the buzzer rang.

Ashley laid down flat, coughing and gasping.

"That's what I'm talking about, girl! *That's* what I'm talking about!" he said again pointing his finger at her repeatedly. "Hooooooooo!!" he howled, throwing his head back, in imitation of the Nature Boy Ric Flair.

Ashley raised a hand and gave a thumbs-up before letting it fall to the mat. It took nearly a minute before her breathing settled back into a recognizable pattern, but once it did, Jake spoke again.

"Alright. Hydrate and take a ten minute break. Then we'll do it again."

"*What?!*" Ashley shouted then began coughing.

"You heard me."

"Same rules?" she asked, hoping for a different response than she got.

"Fuck yeah!"

"Holy shit," she panted in between breaths. "I might as well … roll over now … and just give it to you. Fuck!"

"Well, if that's what you want …" Jake began to walk towards her.

"No! No, no, no!" Ashley held both her hands up, palms out. "Just kidding! *Just* kidding."

"Alright then. Get your ass up and hydrate."

Each round was slightly different, but after a couple more of empty hands only, Jake let her tuck a training blade in her waistband. Things started ending much sooner after that.

Jake roleplayed being a typical bad guy. Someone who didn't have as much training as Jake possessed, and someone whose will to push through pain and focus on winning wasn't as resolved as his own. When Ashley successfully landed an attack, if he thought a normal, motivated attacker would fall or give up, Jake did too. Next, he added a training blade or gun to his hand to start out each scenario and put Ashley at a greater disadvantage, to place more pressure on her and push her to perform beyond what she thought she could do.

To Jake's great pleasure, Ashley managed to find a moment to go for the weapon, nearly hurting him each time … because she was *trying to* every time.

After lunch, Ashley was completely spent but had held her own for each one-minute fight.

"Alright, Ashley. After you finish eating, clean up and lay down. Sleep and rest. I have something big planned for this evening, but don't worry … I *know* you are ready for it." Jake winked at her.

Oh shit, went through Ashley's mind, but her confidence had undergone immense growth. She made it through today. He had even unloaded punches on her a few times, and she was able to cover and deflect it and move to a better position. The ones that slipped through hurt like hell, knocking her silly, but she stayed conscious and got to her blade. "You can handle it," she told herself. "You can handle it, Ashley, whatever it is. Just don't mind-fuck yourself."

*****

Though it was only for a few hours, Ashley slept the sleep of the dead, never moving once after she passed out on the bed. Upon waking, she dressed and walked out and stood in front of the mirror. She had a little bruise on her jaw, but other than that she didn't look any worse for the wear from earlier. She turned to exit out to the bay but realized the door was shut. She went to it, turned the knob, and pushed. It was dead bolted from the other side. *Odd*, she thought, *it hasn't been like this during the day time.* She went back in her room, sat down, and picked up a book to kill the time.

It felt like an hour went by before she heard the door open, and Jake came in. He looked dead serious.

"Alright, girl. Tonight is a moment of truth for you, but a moment I have prepared you for. This will be an opportunity for you to transform yourself into something greater than you have ever been. It's sink or swim, though. Pass or fail. Nothing in between." He paused for a few seconds, then began to speak again.

"There is a man out there. I located him through some perverse dark web chatroom and researched him. He is here to rape you … *viciously.*"

Ashley's mouth dropped open a little.

"I have told him that, for a large sum of money, I could provide such a lady for his purposes. He thinks he is here for a victim, a weak, helpless girl whom he can freely abuse. But that is not you anymore, Ashley. You are a predator. The wolf in sheep's clothing. You must kill him or be violated and victimized. Your choice. Here is your garrote."

He slipped it into her hands.

"Just into the woods, where we shoot the bow and arrow, is your knife. It is laying on the ground next to the tree where you sit and lean when I allow you to rest. If you make it to the lean-to, your bow is there with one arrow. Also, hand me your brush."

Ashley did so. Jake gripped it and pulled the bristle end off, revealing a solid thick plastic shiv tapering to a point. Ashley's eyes opened wide, clearly surprised.

"All along, you've had a weapon and didn't know it, but now you know. Use it if necessary. You will get a twenty second head start, and he will pursue you into the woods. He will have a flashlight as well. Use what I have taught you. Kill him, and you will not be a victim fleeing the hunter. You will be the hunter from this day forth."

Ashley felt numb. She had built up animosity enough to kill Jake, but a complete stranger?

Jake saw the dilemma on her face.

"Look, he is a *bad man*, and he has paid greatly to come here and have his way with you. He intends to rape you in brutal fashion, inflict severe injury and suffering, and then, when he's done playing with his food, make you die a most painful death. If you don't want to suffer this fate you must fight, and you must kill. It is the law of the jungle. Let the beast out. I've seen it in you, Ashley. You can do this."

He looked her over then bent and picked up a case. He pulled out black pants and a dark purple shirt with violet accents along with a belt and some black low top tennis shoes.

"Here, you must wear these instead."

He handed them to her and walked out without another word. Ashley changed, pocketed the garrote, then sat and waited, praying quietly for victory but not forgiveness for what she intended to do.

*****

When Jake led her outside, the man was standing there. He was decently fit but nowhere near Jake's size or build. He had a sickness in his eyes. Eyes like a rabid animal ready to attack. He looked her up and down and flicked his tongue at her but did not say a word. It made Ashley want to rip his throat out, but she had learned, "Deception is the highest

50

form of Warfare," from reading Sun Tzu's *Art of War* and from all her training and fighting with Jake. She played the frightened maiden, crying, snotting, and trembling, feigning desperate, terrified glances.

Jake looked at the man and asked him if he was ready, and he nodded.

"Twenty seconds on the clock, mister. Alright you dirty whore, get ready to run! In three ... two ... one, GO!"

Ashley took off for the wood line, escaping the light of the campfire right away as she cut behind a large tree and ran straight ahead for where her knife would be.

The rabid man cried out behind her, "Run little girl! Run! Cause you're gonna *squeeeeal* like a piglet when I shove my way inside you! SOOOUUUUIIIIIEEEEEEE!"

"Ten seconds," Jake shouted as Ashley knelt and found her knife. Her eyes were adjusting to the dark already. Her spirit was calm, focused on the task ahead. She was a predator now, not the panicked, weak rabbit, frozen in fear on the night Jake took her, so overcome by violence that she couldn't summon one ounce of resistance. That wasn't her now, though. It never would be again, either.

She took off for the lean-to, moving with a purpose —a purpose that would likely have no option but to end with this man's death. Ashley was fine with that.

A few seconds later, Jake shouted again.

"Release the hound!"

The man would be on his way now, she told herself. She had three close range weapons she could finish him with, but she would prefer to stick an arrow in him and then move in for the kill.

The man trotted slowly along the forest floor, waving the flashlight back and forth, calling out to her, his ego apparently sure he was the predator here.

"Come on, little piggy! Where are ya?! Don't be shy! Willard here's got nothing but a *stiff rod* waiting for your tender touch."

Ashley was tempted to think it would be easy to kill him but didn't want to underestimate her opponent.

When she reached the lean-to and found the bow, she took the time to secure the knife and sheath to her belt with some 550 cord Jake had left for her. The hairbrush she stuffed bristles first into her back pocket. She could hear the man moving roughly in her direction, but perhaps not quite on an intersecting path. As she stared in his direction, she could see the light bobbing to the right of her, around thirty feet lateral of her position and about fifty yards out. She knelt down quickly and dug into the hole where she cooked food at times. There was wood ash in there. She smeared a handful all over her face and arms to help further blend into the dark. Then she picked up the bow, knocked the arrow, and began moving quietly off to her left on a flanking course.

Now *she* was the hunter stalking him.

"Come on out, little pig!" the man yelled, waving the flashlight back and forth. "Or I'll huff, and I'll puff, and I'll BLOW your panties right off!!" The man let out a cackling laugh when he was done, pleased with his comedic improvisation.

Ashley maneuvered to where she was even with him. She squatted to pick up a piece of limb and threw it out in front of where he was now. He immediately shined his light and started off in that direction. Ashley used the noise he was making to enable her to move quicker and get behind him. She knelt and drew the arrow back. She could see his outline ahead, about twenty yards away. He was standing still but turning back and forth quickly, searching with the light. Twice, she took a deep breath, held it, and breathed out with control. The third inhale she held it in, timing the rotation of his torso. Once he was in position, she exhaled. When her lungs were nearly empty and her chest relaxed, she released the arrow. She heard the arrow make a faint whistling noise, then a thump. A fraction of a second later the man's scream ripped the night.

Ashley dropped the bow, drew her knife, and sprinted toward the wailing curses.

"FUUUUCK! What the fuck is going on, man? Something's stuck in my shoulder!"

Dammit! thought Ashley. *I at least hoped it would be a lung, if not his heart.*

She was almost on top of him when he turned around and held the light under his chin, staggering back and forth. She came to a stop about seven yards away.

"Here! Here I am! Help me!" the man cried out, thinking the footsteps approaching from behind him belonged to Jake.

"I'm not here to help you, you demented fuck!"

The man shoved the light forward, pointing it right at her, illuminating her whole body for him to see. It was the same clothes, but the face streaked and smudged with ash caused him to jump.

"Who the fuck *are* you?" he asked, perplexed.

"A righteous fucking predator," she said with a calm confidence. "That's what."

Ashley cut right and sprinted behind some trees, out of the light, then dropped to the ground and began a rapid low crawl before shifting into a crouch several feet away from where she disappeared. She scooped up a stick off the forest floor, jumped up and threw it at him. The stick struck the flashlight, knocking it out of his hand. Without hesitation, Ashley fell upon the wounded prey like a lioness in all her glory.

The blade drove straight down through his clavicle well, piercing the subclavian artery and causing him to drop to his knees. She wrenched the knife back and forth, then, without withdrawing the blade, she cut out across his throat, severing both carotids, jugulars, and his windpipe in one brutal motion. Blood pumped and jetted through the air beneath the moonlight, covering her and the forest floor around them. He clutched his throat with his good hand, the other hanging useless at his side. Within seconds, he became too dizzy to stay vertical and fell face-first to the ground and rolled onto his back staring up at Ashley as she stared into his eyes and squatted down next to him.

"Don't you die yet, you sick fuck!" she screamed in his face, spittle flying. The knife rose and descended into his groin, again and again, piercing his flaccid penis and testicles in multiplicity. If he could have, he would have screamed in tremendous pain.

Ashley turned her attention to his face. Shifting the blade into a forward grip, she pressed the point into one eye at a time and flicked the blade sideways, laying his eye balls wide open. His whole body writhed with each cut.

Her breathing was deep, but oxygen was reaching the muscles more than the brain. She was primal now, a beast released. The hate she built up over the past two months was being vented on this man. After ravaging his manhood and his lustful eyes, she wanted to shut him up symbolically as well. She raised the blade, icepick style, one last time and stabbed him right in the mouth, the blade penetrating between his lips, through his tongue, and into the back of his throat till it stopped against the cervical spine.

Thick crimson filled his mouth, bubbling out over his lips as they opened and closed like a fish out of water, his body still involuntarily trying to breathe. The gurgling noises he made would have disgusted Ashley if he were an innocent person. Instead, she took joy in them and mocked his death. Opening and closing her mouth in a vulgar imitation of his final struggles, she ridiculed his last moments until his attempts to inhale became shallower and stopped.

He's done, she told herself.

She withdrew the knife and stood, turning to face the house. She threw her head back and screamed. Unadulterated rage composed every sound wave careening through the forest.

"JAAAAAAAAKE!" She took a deep breath, filling her lungs for the war cry. "I'M COMING FOR YOU! WHERE ARE YOU, YOU SICK MOTHERFUCKER?!"

"Right here, babe," he said calmly. A green dot appeared on her chest.

"CRACK!"

Ashley went rigid, then dropped the knife and made a gurgling cry as she fell sideways to the ground like a tree chopped down. Her body seized up like an epileptic, made rigid by the electric current flowing through her system. Jake made a hurried approach, wearing the night vision goggles. He kicked away the knife and knelt beside her, a syringe in his other hand. As soon as the taser's current ceased, he injected her with the sedative then stepped back, keeping his finger on the trigger in case he needed to hit her again.

He only had to pull the trigger one more time.

*****

Ashley woke the next morning lying on her bed wearing only undergarments. Raising up, she sat on the edge of the mattress and tried to wade through the thick haze filling her mind. She glanced down at her hands and saw the dry blood covering them. There was never a doubt in her mind she had done it. She remembered it all. Including the taser.

55

She fingered the small holes where the electrodes pierced her flesh, one on her upper thigh and the other where it hit her breast. *Damn near through my nipple*, she thought.

"That pussy," she muttered, thinking how she was robbed of a chance to kill Jake.

She stood, slow and cautious, establishing her balance, then walked into the bathroom and looked in the small mirror. Her face and neck were still covered in blood and ash. Her eyes were different though. Her countenance stone. She made herself smile, but it still looked wrong, replaced by something cynical and esoteric. She had eaten of the tree of knowledge, and it showed.

Turning on the shower, she climbed in, scrubbed off thoroughly, then filled the tub and soaked, her mind drifting into an abyss, an ocean of Zen nothingness.

Time melted and flowed with the waves she drifted on until the knock came, dragging her back to shore.

"Yes?" she called out, monotone and disinterested.

"Time to get dressed and meet me out here. Clothes are on your bed."

Without another word, Jake left. She could hear his footsteps fade away. She lingered for another minute then exited the tub and dried off. She saw the clothes, but there was no breakfast like usual. She dressed and brushed her hair. She couldn't believe he left the brush with her. An oversight? She wasn't sure, but she tucked it in her hoodie pocket before walking out into the bay. When she exited the door, she stopped in her tracks.

Ashley's mouth went slack, eyes squinting. Her whole head jutted forward to determine if what she was seeing was real or some hallucination. She was betting on hallucination. She blinked three times and screwed her knuckles into both eyes.

Nope, still there, she thought.

56

Straight ahead, tied to a chair was a man she had not seen in years. A man whose influence upon her life could *not* be understated.

It was her Uncle Tim.

Fear clawed at Ashley's stomach, but only for a moment. She was made of sterner stuff now. Anxiety found no purchase. Panic could find no way in.

Ashley scrutinized him. He was out of shape, trapped like a rabbit in a snare, terrified. He couldn't threaten her anymore. She had ascended the food chain and stood head and shoulders above him now.

He stared in Ashley's direction. Recognition had not dawned on him yet. He continued to scan her features as she walked towards him.

"Ashley?" he asked at last, his tone incredulous. She didn't answer him, just continued walking forward. The closer she got, the more confident he grew in his initial recognition.

"Oh my god! Ashley! It's you! What are you doing here?"

Ashley's heart was pumping faster, uncertain of Jake's intentions. She didn't even respond to Uncle Tim. She stopped about six feet away from him then looked over his shoulder to stare Jake in the eye. He was standing inside the cage, the door shut.

"What the *fuck* is this all about, Jake?" Her delivery was abrupt and demanding, her eyes a knife to his neck, threatening for an honest response.

"It's really very simple Ashley. He ruined your childhood. He crippled your adult life. He made you a victim and abused you over and over. Even after you escaped, the damage couldn't be erased ... until now."

"You want me to kill him?" she said flatly.

"Fuck, girl. Don't *you*?" Jake threw it out there and just looked at her as if he was looking *inside* her to make sure there wasn't some alien creature hiding there.

The staring contest dragged out in silence for several seconds until Ashley finally lowered her gaze and stared at Uncle Tim with crocodile eyes.

Tim met her gaze and saw beyond it. Seeing the change in her soul, panic gripped him.

"Ashley!" he cried. "You can't kill me. It's wrong!"

"WRONG?!" Her voice jumped multiple octaves, righteous anger erupting inside. She let out a short, spontaneous laugh. "Wrong?" she said bluntly, shaking her head. She lunged forward, grabbed him by his coat lapels, and snatched hard, pulling his face close to hers, his wrist and ankles stretching at the bonds.

A lion roared from inside her.

"What's WRONG is raping a little girl! What's WRONG was making me suck your cock all those nights and telling me it was what good nieces did for their uncles! THAT is fucking wrong! All those years of abuse, all the damage done. I never knew how badly you fucked my mind up till now. But I'm not fucked up anymore! YOU HEAR ME?! I'm not that weak little girl anymore. I'm STRONG!"

She screamed the last words at the top of her lungs an inch from his face then pushed him back into the chair. She stood over him, took a deep breath, held it, then blew it out with force, an unconscious expression of frustration and rage.

"And you're still just a sick bastard who needs to be put down like a rabid dog." She hocked and spit on his lap then turned around and marched for the table where the knife lay; the one she had killed the pigs with. She picked it up in a forward grip, and moved her hand up and down the handle, letting the wrist go with the weight of it, judging the hacking power. She turned around and walked back towards her uncle.

"That's it, Ashley! Do it, and you'll be free!" Jake gripped the cage fence with his fingers, his face pressed against it, a titillating anticipation painting his entire appearance; vibrant and feral, a one-man Coliseum crowd and emperor combined, cheering her on while simultaneously giving the thumbs down.

Ashley pointed the blade at Jake with an outstretched arm and barked.

"Don't you *dare* tell me what to *do*! This is MY CHOICE! ALL MINE!"

Jake let go of the cage and moved back, a small but sinister smile creeping across his face.

Ashley was in control now. No one else. She walked over to Tim's left side; grabbed his fingers and uncurled them till they were straight. "Keep your hand open. You understand?" Tim nodded understanding while begging at the same time.

"Please, Ashley. Don't do this."

"*Shut. Your. Mouth.* You do not have the *right* to talk to me." Her words were venom from a spitting cobra. Uncle Tim shut up and hoped for the best. There was no reasoning with her, he believed.

"This is the hand you always held my head down with, no matter how much I tried to pull away or cried, it didn't matter. You told me I'd get used to it. *Used to it.*" She shook her head, and turned away from him, looking over her right shoulder. When she turned back, the blade fell.

Three fingers dropped to the concrete together. The index finger leaned at an adverse angle, half severed.

Uncle Tim's scream pierced the quiet and reverberated off the metal walls and vaulted ceiling of the bay.

Ashley's face was blank, a stoic canvas of indifference to his pain.

Blood jetted from the tiny stumps as Ashley hacked twice more, removing index finger and thumb completely. Uncle Tim howled as Ashley looked around, searching for something. She quickly spotted the claw hammer and retrieved it, shifting the blade to her left hand and gripping the hammer with her right.

"And this," she said, pointing at his groin with the hammer, "this was the instrument of all my torture ... but not anymore."

She slammed the hammer down on his crotch, just one powerful swing. His eyes rolled back, and his body tried to straighten out rigid. He couldn't scream. He couldn't breathe. He just twisted his head back and forth, overcome by the pain. Ashley leaned in towards his face.

"Uncle Tim? Look at me," she said softly, but he didn't respond. "LOOK AT ME!" Her hand flew through the air, striking his cheek open handed. "Look at me!" His eyes fluttered back down, and he gritted his teeth. Her eyes locked with his right before his head bowed, and he vomited in his own lap.

"Ugh. That's fucking gross," Ashley exclaimed. "But you know what Uncle Tim? That's just your weakness. It profits you nothing." Ashley delighted in turning Jake's phrase he used on her that first night on her uncle instead.

"I want you to feel my pain ... my frailty ... my helplessness as a child on all those nights, the inevitable reality, knowing I was dying a little bit each time. I want you to feel that ... right now, as the pain engulfs you ... and you bleed to death."

She slid the blade into his abdomen slowly, just above the naval, and pushed until she felt it stop on his spine. For an eternity she just held it there, staring him in the eyes.

"I'm sorry," he sputtered, blood appearing in his mouth. Ashley twisted the blade sideways and leveraged it back and forth, making sure she penetrated the descending aorta.

"It's ok, Uncle Tim, maybe God will forgive you." She kissed him on the head, pulled the blade out, and walked away.

Jake's cooler sat by the table. She walked over, sat the hammer down, and reached inside to retrieve a beer. She wished it was hard liquor, but it would do. She popped the top and leaned on the table, drinking and watching Uncle Tim as he bled out, the blade held limply at her side. She didn't have to wait long.

After a couple of minutes, Jake exited the cage and pressed his fingers to Tim's neck to check for a pulse. Nothing.

"Your uncle's dead," Jake said bluntly.

"What now?" she said. "Is the end nigh? Time for our finale? Last dance at the ball?" Ashley let out an uneasy laugh and looked down at her beer.

"That's up to you, Ashley. It's always been up to you."

"So," the sarcasm dripped from her tongue, "what are my 'choices', *Jake*?" She glared at him as she spoke his name then tilted the beer back and guzzled the rest.

"Well, basically, on one hand, if you really, REALLY, want to try to kill me, we can dance that dance, but … you really should know by now you can't survive that one, not with me. I'm not the standard fare, ego-driven male relying on strength and intimidation over the weak. I'm an apex predator. I train to hunt the hunters. You are too, now, if you didn't connect those dots yet. But you're not at my level. Not yet. That would take years of training. If you come at me, head on, and I go at you, full on, you'll be a dead lioness *real* quick. That's just the reality of it. However," Jake tipped his beer in Ashley's direction, "on the other hand, if you can detach and look at the last two months of your life objectively, what have I really done to you Ashley? Did I rape you? Did I victimize you beyond the first night when I had to make you think I would hurt you if you didn't obey me? Just what did I do to you?"

He paused to let her process his words before continuing on.

Ashley felt a righteous rage flare inside her chest, swelling until her eyes kindled with an unquenchable fire at Jake's total dismissal of the suffering and humiliation he had put her through. It was a slap in the face. He had stolen weeks of her life she would never get back. He had enslaved her free will to obey him no matter what. The stress alone of knowing that at the end of all this she would have to fight a win or die battle with him was an ever-present thorn in her mind.

Jake didn't care one lick what Ashley thought, though. "Wolves don't care what sheep think," she had read in an article he left in her room. Jake felt above it all. He had his own justifications.

"I'll tell you what I did. I made you strong. I crushed the weakness in you and gave you all the keys to all your cages so you could open the doors and set *yourself* free."

Jake spread his arms wide, looked around and smirked, as if his observations were matter of fact and impossible to miss.

"I facilitated one of the greatest prison breaks a person could ever witness. And here you stand, escaped from your personal Alcatraz, a monument to the resiliency and adaptability of the human spirit when it's pushed beyond its past defeats and self-imposed limitations. And if you want to walk away a free woman you can do just that," he said, pointing at the door.

"I'll drug you so you don't know how to get to my

place, then carry you back to your civilization and drop you off. Pretty much like setting a wounded animal free again once it's healed up, except now you're a carnivore instead of a lowly old herbivore."

Jake chuckled at the analogy and smiled.

Ashley stared at him, wishing she had laser vision. She'd burn his eyes right out of their sockets and punch a hole through the back of his skull if she could. She *hated* him. More than she could ever find words to express. And she really, REALLY wanted to kill him. At the same time, as her brain whirred and clicked, cogs turning to fall in place, she began to realize the gift he had bestowed on her. No matter how twisted his logic and despicable his methods … she *was* free. But if she tried him, head on, she knew she'd die. *Patience and deception*, she thought. Then repeated it in her mind like a mantra.

She laid the knife on the table, stood and started walking towards him with a slow, deliberate swagger, arms at her side, hands held away from her thighs, palms facing him.

"You know I fucking hate you," she stated. "And I *really, REALLY* do want to kill you. But I'm free, and I don't want to die before I get a chance to live that freedom. So, I guess I'll take option two." She was within six feet of him when she stopped and waited for the next step.

"So, what now, boss?

Jake shook his head and breathed a sigh of relief. He didn't want to kill her. She was his greatest success yet.

"Well, let's get that shot in you then you can quick wash your hands and change your clothes. When you wake up, you'll be back in Kansas, metaphorically speaking." He winked at her.

"OK. Let's do it. I'm ready to get the fuck up out of here."

Jake turned his back halfway on her and directed his gaze to the table where a syringe laid. It was a second, maybe two, but it was all Ashley needed.

She reached in the large hoodie pocket with both hands and withdrew the brush shiv, stripping the bristle portion off and leaving it in the pocket as she did so. She rocketed forward stabbing him in his left kidney, causing his back to bow reflexively away from the pain. Her left hand grabbed his clothing at the left shoulder as she continued to stab him, once, twice more.

Jake spun to his left, turning to the outside of her gripping hand and slapped her left shoulder, spinning her in front of him and moving the weapon offline of his body. He had bought himself a moment of safety, Ashley unable to freely stab him without turning into him first.

Jake capitalized on that beat in time, his right hand trapping the wrist of the hand Ashley held the knife with. With his other hand, he peeled her head back, slamming her to the floor. Ashley tried to figure out what had just happened. One second she was looking at the world horizontally, the next she was looking up at it. Before she could orient herself and move, one knee was on her face, pinning her head. The other knee was crushing Ashley's forearm, weakening her grip on the brush handle.

"God *damn*, you've become a feisty, *sneaky* bitch! Learned your lessons well, you did!"

Jake's face contorted in pain.

"Janet! Bring the stronger dose sedative. Sally, standby with the taser. Rachel, baby, please stop the bleeding in my back. The combat gauze is sitting right there in that toolbox. Roxanne, do me a favor and strip that brush out of her hand then straddle her feet and hold her knees flat."

Four women came out of their hiding spots, moving as a unit, each performing the duties requested. Ashley saw two of them as they approached from her left. They had nice figures, fit and pretty, and they were dressed in regular clothes, but they both were wearing masks.

Perhaps this is a ball after all, Ashley thought.

The masks were typical for the Masquerade balls she had read about from the 18th century. One was white with pearls and golden feathers framing it, a teardrop jewel beneath one eye. The other was covered with black feathers and had a yellow beak. They moved beyond her limited field of view. Ashley lost track of them but soon felt their presence. A knee dropped on her wrist. The brush was peeled away while another girl straddled her legs, hugging them with her own to restrain Ashley's lower body.

Jake spoke in a calm tone to Ashley, now.

"Just stay still, Ashley. I won't hurt you. I love you. Just like I love them."

"Jake, she really stabbed you good. We're going to need to call Hector to stitch you up. This is beyond my skills."

"What the fuck is going on?" she managed to spit out. "Who are they?" Ashley gritted through the pain and pressure of Jake's knee on the side of her head and jaw.

"They're my ladies and my lovers and my best friends, Ash. They're ones that I freed like you … but they came back."

She felt the shot go in. A few seconds later the world started to spin and darken.

"I got you, Jake. I got you real good," she mumbled.

"Yes, you did, Ash. Yes, you did."

"You'd be bleeding to death right now if not for these bitches."

"I know Ash. I know. Guess I'm lucky to have some good women who love me."

"I got you, Jake ... you know I did ... and ... and we're even ... I ain't ever ... ever coming back ..."

Ashley's voice trailed off as the sedative eased her into oblivion. The last thing she saw was a masked lady with an empty syringe in one hand lie down and prop herself up on her elbows, a silver version of the traditional theatre mask with its tragic sad face looking at her, head tilted. The masked lady held one hand up, fingers rolling up and down in succession, over and over like the endless tide, waving goodbye to Ashley.

*****

Ashley woke to the morning sun burning bright in her eyes. She was reclined in the driver's seat of her car, keys in the ignition, engine running to keep her warm. On the seat next to her was the knife she had killed Uncle Tim with, but cleaned. Her shiv brush and garrote sat next to them as well as the stack of books from her room. A piece of folded paper sat beneath. She opened it, and a fake ID with her picture and a debit card fell out. She read the typed print on the paper.

> *"The debit card is linked to an account that holds the $200,000 the man paid to try to rape you. The ID ensures you can access it. Be careful what you tell the police. Uncle Tim's death was recorded. When you're ready to come home, we'll know. We all come home eventually.*
> *—The Girls"*

Ashley sat there for some time, planning how she would handle her return. What would she say to the police and her family? She couldn't tell them the truth. She supposed she would have to just go with the standard fare—

rape, physical and mental abuse, and routine sedation. She would tell them she had no idea why the man returned her. Of course, that would never explain how she had gained muscle and hardened her body or how she acquired the skills she now possessed. She would have to come up with an explanation for the former and hide the latter. She sat up, put the car in drive, and headed home. As an afterthought, she made a mental note to stash the weapons before calling the police.

*****

Chaos ensued from the moment she hit send on the burner phone Jake left in her pocket. Officers, family, and friends invaded her life. Media crawled like ants about her house for days. Everyone shook their head in astonishment because the man had let her go, and they all wanted to treat her like a helpless victim. It made her nauseous and stirred her heart to violence.

She had to leave the presence of those people, including family, before she lashed out.

No one understood what she now knew to be truth. They were sheep to her. Weak, ignorant, bleating sheep … and she hated them with a newfound passion. All her life she had been one of the flock, volunteering to spend her days in a recurring cycle of slaughter. Her own personhood and needs had been subservient to the predators demanding her life satiate their own desires. She truly hated who she had been, and to her, the more she considered it, the enablers were worse than Jake had ever been.

In the coming days, she missed the training. She sought out various martial arts schools but couldn't stand the false bravado and fanciful application of techniques. She wanted the brutal, the effective, not sport tactics bullshit; she wanted to be pushed, to be tested.

School after school she went to failed to meet her expectations. She was chastised for using too much force on more than one occasion. Theoretical didn't cut it for her. She wanted battle-proven techniques. Drilling was great and refined the skills, but at some point, she had to be challenged to apply those skills under duress. She wanted people to come at her hard, but the guys all treated her with kid gloves, and if she fired hard on them they would just chastise her and tell her to relax.

Her family and friends didn't recognize her anymore. She had been altered on a drastic scale. There was a huge wall between them, a gaping chasm they could not cross. It was as if she had left a 110 outlet and returned a 220. They were so different connection wasn't even a possibility any longer. Ashley drifted away from them within a month or two.

She threw herself into her schoolwork but had to get a different job; something far away from the prying eyes of the public. Telemarketing seemed a good fit for a time. She could practice manipulating people in conversation.

Every day, she felt further and further divided from mankind. An aberration. Unable to think like they did. Unable to breathe the lies they survived on, constantly having to abandon their gatherings before she suffocated.

She searched social media and found some people who thought like her but still, she could never tell her story, never fully connect with them. She longed to find a place she could belong, but could ultimately only think of one.

Months passed, then one day she arrived home from school and checked her mailbox. There was a folded piece of paper with typed print inside.

"We see your misery, your search for acceptance.
Are you ready to come home?
—Jake and the Girls"

Ashley glanced around, wondering if they were nearby watching, then stood still, staring at the letter for some time. More than once, in times of quiet reflection, she had considered the prospect of returning. She stared off in space at the coffee shop or lay in bed thinking about who she used to be, who she was now, and how she got here. Ashley considered the things she missed, imagining what life would be like with Jake and the Girls. What would it be like to have a place where she belonged? To be amongst people with whom secrets were unnecessary and she was accepted for who she was now?

She pulled out a pen and scribbled one word on the page then folded the letter and placed it back in the mailbox.

That one word?

"ALMOST."

THE END

Acknowledgements

I would like to thank everyone who has been of immense help to me in this process: my wife for supporting all my writing efforts, my friends who beta read this short novella and gave me their feedback in a very timely fashion, and all my author friends on Facebook who have so kindly and freely offered advice. Thank you, everyone, sincerely.

Fragment of
Mike Duke's *LOW*

NOVEMBER 1, 10:00 A.M.

"Officer Adams, my client, Johnny Greene, swears that you planted that crack pipe in his pocket, but I know better than to think that is true with the reputation for integrity you have. If by some chance it wasn't his, it was probably one of his friends that slid it in there. He's an idiot for even suggesting you would do such a thing, and I'm not going to pursue that line of questioning. However, he insists on testifying, despite my objections. In fact, the bastard threatened me earlier if I didn't let him testify. As far as I'm concerned, the stupid fucker can hang himself."

Chad Bigleby hated the days when he had to take his turn at being a public defender. Adams nodded in acknowledgement and chuckled a little, his face showing he felt Chad's pain.

"So basically, my only point of contention will be with the validity of the pat-down. Since his aunt lives in the same project where you stopped and interviewed him, this could give him a valid reason for being in the neighborhood, and he wouldn't have been trespassing. Did you ask for consent to search my client?"

Adams was completely candid.

"No, sir, I sure didn't. Based on the time of day and the location being known for its high drug traffic and numerous shots-fired calls, I felt it was necessary to ensure the safety of my partner and myself."

"Humph. The judge might agree with you on that. I guess we'll see. Thank you for your honesty, Officer Adams."

"Of course."

Adams stared at his watch every five minutes for the next hour until the case was finally called. He did not want to be late for his and Amy's counseling session.

The longer Chad sat and waited, the more he stewed over Johnny having the audacity to threaten him. He decided to show Johnny who was in control of whom here.

"Commonwealth vs. Greene."

Adams approached the stand and gave his testimony, recounting who, what, when, where, how, and why. When finished, the judge spoke.

"Your witness, Mr. Bigleby."

"Thank you, Your Honor. Good day, Officer Adams."

"Good day to you, sir."

"I just have a couple of questions, Officer Adams. Let me see if I have this right. You're saying that you stopped my client in a known drug area and that, upon patting him down you felt something that, based on your training and experience, you believed to be a crack pipe?"

"That's correct, sir."

"And you found this in the right pocket of Mr. Greene's jacket?"

"Yes sir. The right pocket."

"And the lab results showed that it tested positive for cocaine?"

"Yes, sir."

"Your Honor, I have no further questions of the officer at this time, though I would like to reserve the right to redirect after my client's testimony."

The judge looked slightly puzzled, but agreed. Adams recognized Chad's game plan.

"I call Mr. Greene to the stand, Your Honor," Chad smiled as he did so.

"Mr. Greene, before Officer Adams stopped you, was there a crack pipe in your jacket pocket?"

"No, sir."

"Well, how do you think it got there?"

"Officer Adams put it there while he was patting me down."

"Why do you think he did that?"

"Because he's crooked, and he don't like me. We've had words before."

"Those words, that would be the last time you got arrested for cocaine possession, wouldn't it?"

"Uh, yeah."

Johnny's face looked confused, not tracking where Chad was going.

"And you were convicted of that charge, weren't you?"

He paused, and looked at the judge, then glanced around briefly.

"Um, yes. I was."

"But you're positive that Officer Adams put that crack pipe in your pocket?"

"Absolutely."

"Can you think of any other way it could have gotten in your jacket pocket?"

"Nope."

"Very well. Your Honor, I'm done with this witness."

"Mr. Grant. The witness is yours," the judge declared.

The Commonwealth Attorney was trying not to smirk as he spoke.

"Your Honor, I have no questions of the witness."

Chad spoke up. "Your Honor, I'd like to call Officer Adams back to the stand."

Officer Adams strolled back up and sat down, trying not to laugh.

"Officer Adams, is there any truth to my client's claim that you planted that crack pipe on his person?"

Adams looked right at Johnny.

"Not one bit, sir."

"Of course not. I expected as much. Officer Adams, I have no further questions, and I thank you for your service and dedication to our city. Good day. Your Honor, the Defense rests."

Adams winked at Johnny then left the stand.

"Your Honor, the Prosecution rests as well," Mr. Grant declared.

The guilty verdict came quickly and the guards led Johnny out of the courtroom before it could even dawn on him what just happened. Chad nodded to Officer Adams and the Commonwealth Attorney, looking innocent as could be.

Find more at

Mike's *LOW*

https://books2read.com/low

https://www.amazon.com/Low-Mike-Duke-ebook/dp/
B075VQ5W5R/

Stitched Smile Publications

https://www.stitchedsmilepublications.com/

About The Author

Mike was a cop for almost 12 years, but the last 12 years he's been teaching Military, Law Enforcement and Bodyguards high speed, tactical and off-road driving as well as hand to hand Combatives. He enjoys martial arts and has been a practitioner since 1989 of various styles. Filipino blade arts are his current favorite. Since he was a teenager he's loved reading, writing, and watching movies, particularly in the horror and sci-fi genre. He's also been a prolific reader of theology and studied quite extensively for a layman. He has a beautiful wife who is very supportive and a son and daughter who are both graduated. His babies now are a German Shepherd named Ziva, a Daddy's girl who loves to play... even when he's writing, and a Border Collie mix named Joey "The Bandit" who will steal anything and everything he can, even the toys right out of Ziva's mouth. Mike is a lover of music as well and it is an integral part of his writing ritual.

Mike writes an eclectic mix of horror stories. He explores dark supernatural entities, cosmic terrors, and natural monstrosities. However, the wicked deeds the human heart can conceive and inflict on others as well as our capacity to act against such things pervades much of his work. According to Chris Hall, at DLS Reviews, Mike is "a master of utterly uncompromising hardboiled revenge-thrillers." He has a way of provoking a significant response from his readers – whether shock, terror, dread, an uneasy sense of empathy, Heebie Jeebie crawlies or surprise at unexpected twists. Mike will make you feel while you read his words. Afterwards, the potential horrors of twisted moral visions, the deplorable nature of humanity's vices and weaknesses, the possibility of unearthly and supernatural threats and the plausibility of the hideous within the normal; all these things will consciously disturb and haunt you, attempting to take root in your mind and make you question what you know and believe. For how long? Take a read and find out.

His latest works are the novel *LOW* from Stitched Smiles Publications and the novella *Warm, Dark Places are Best*, which he self-published. His most well-known work thus far is his first, a novella entitled *Ashley's Tale*. Stitched Smiles Publications will be republishing *Ashley's Tale* and part two, *Ashley's Tale: Making Jake*, in August 2018, along with part three of the series, *Ashley's Tale: The Initiation*, which will be novel length. Duke also has another novel slated for release through Stitched Smile Publications in October 2018 – a cosmic horror story entitled *Where the Gods Sleep*. Look for Duke's short stories in multiple anthologies coming out in the latter part of 2018 as well.

Made in the USA
Middletown, DE
20 July 2019